The Bradford Family ADVENTURES

Big Trouble at the Beach

by

Jerry B. Jenkins

MOODY PRESS
CHICAGO

To Tom Cappelen, Pat, Tommy, and Timmy

Contents

1

The Outing

Neither Daniel nor Yolanda Bradford had ever been on the beach of the Atlantic Ocean late at night. It was mysterious and beautiful.

"Oh, Daniel," Yolanda said, "isn't it pretty?"

Daniel was almost scared. But he wouldn't have missed this for anything. His parents and older brother and sister, Jim and Maryann, had enjoyed the ocean at night before. So they had stayed by the steep bluffs. They promised to be there when Daniel and Yolanda returned from their stroll down the beach.

Yolanda kept looking back and waving. She was always reassured to know that the rest of the family was still there. Even Daniel found himself checking once in a while when Yolanda didn't. But soon they went around a bend and were out of sight of their parents, Maryann, and Jim.

"We'd better get back, huh?" Yolanda said.

"Nah. In a little while. This is great."

It had been a scorching day, over a hundred degrees as they rolled along in a rented camper toward the East Coast. Now it was near midnight and much cooler, but not cold. A high, white moon illuminated the water and the sand. Daniel stopped walking. He kicked off his shoes and socks and rolled up his pants.

"What're you doing, Dan?" Yolanda asked.

"Just gotta test the water," he said. "Listen to it."

The waves slapping against the shore, a light breeze, and some faraway birds were all they could hear.

"Hold your breath," Yolanda suggested. "Then all you can hear is the silence."

That almost made Daniel laugh. His little sister had always had her own way of saying things. She removed her sandals and joined him. They stepped carefully near the waterline where the waves seemed to roll higher and higher with each trip to the shore.

"Daniel! Yo-Yo!" came the high, echoing call of their mother. "Time to go!"

"In a minute!" Daniel called back. He boldly stepped into the water and almost yelped. It was so cold! He couldn't figure that out. The sun had been so high and so hot all day. You'd have thought it could warm the whole ocean.

He danced around until he got used to it a little. Yolanda joined him.

"Ooh!" she squealed. "I love it!"

They walked back to the rest of the family. Daniel warned Yolanda to be careful to avoid stepping on any of the night creatures that scurried along in the sand. Yolanda laughed. She said she didn't believe him, but she watched her steps carefully.

"We've got to get to bed," Mrs. Bradford said as everyone piled into the camper. "The Hubers will be here at the crack of dawn, ready for seven big days of fun."

Mr. Bradford wheeled the big vehicle away from the beach. They climbed the steep road to the giant cabin they had rented for both families. Everybody pitched in, and all the food and supplies were unloaded in just a few minutes.

Daniel was tired. But before he joined Jim in the small bedroom in the loft, he answered Yolanda's question about the Hubers again. She was eager to meet them. It seemed that she just couldn't hear enough about them in advance.

"Dad and Mom know Mr. and Mrs. Huber from college?"

Daniel nodded. "Uh-huh. We're not really related. But we're allowed to call them by their first names if we put Uncle or Aunt in front of it."

"Which one's which?" Yolanda asked, laughing at her own joke.

"The Mr. is the uncle, Uncle Steve. And the Mrs. is the aunt, Aunt Carolyn."

"How old are the twins again?"

"Twelve. Tom and Theresa. Both have hair almost as dark as yours. But of course their skin is much lighter. Last year they loved to play games and swim and go exploring."

"I hope they want to this year, too," Yolanda said.

"Me, too."

But they didn't. When the Huber family arrived at six o'clock in the morning, they weren't in good moods. They had left their home two hours before, and it was obvious none of them had had enough sleep.

They were sort of quiet as they unloaded their stuff and got settled in. The adults seemed to be happy enough to see the Bradfords, but the twins seemed embarrassed or shy or something. Daniel couldn't understand it. And not even his bubbly older sister, Maryann, could get them to say much.

"Looking forward to school in the fall?" she asked.

Tom shrugged. Theresa shook her head.

As soon as breakfast was over, Daniel and Yolanda were ready to head for the beach. But the twins took their books and magazines and settled into the couch and a chair in the big, lazy living room that overlooked the ocean.

Mr. Bradford suggested a time of Bible reading and prayer before everyone went their separate ways. The twins dragged themselves back to the breakfast table, still carrying their reading material. They looked bored.

The Hubers had to force the twins to join Daniel and

Yolanda at the beach. Even then they just sat on their towels reading and talking. It was clear that they considered the slightly younger Daniel and Yolanda as nuisances.

Daniel remembered that they had been friendlier and happier the year before. They had included him in their adventures around the beach. "You guys want to go exploring like we did last year?" he suggested.

Theresa didn't even look up from her teen magazine. Tom said something sarcastic. Yolanda had given up on the Huber kids. She was playing by herself in the sand at the water's edge.

Daniel was frustrated. Already he was sure it was going to be hotter even than the day before. It would be the kind of day during which he loved to go hiking and exploring and charging down to the water every hour or so to cool off.

Finally he looked for Jim and Maryann to see what he could do about the Huber twins. He found them in the cabin helping the adults tidy up before they all went to the beach. Their plan was always the same. They got the cabin in perfect shape after each meal. Then they spent several hours at the beach, chatting and playing games. Every night they would go out to dinner, while Jim and Maryann stayed with Daniel and Yo-Yo and the twins.

Daniel huddled in the corner with his brother and sister. Maryann looked at Jim. "What would think of the old Tom Sawyer trick?" she asked.

Jim smiled and nodded. Daniel looked puzzled.

"Oh, you know, Dan," Jim said. "Remember in *Tom Sawyer* when Tom didn't want to have to whitewash the fence all by himself? He made it look like so much fun that everyone else wanted to get in on it? He stood there making a masterpiece out of it until a few friends wanted to try it, too. Soon, he was just standing there supervising while everyone else was painting the fence."

"But I don't want them to do anything for me," Daniel said. "I just want them to be like they were last year. Now they're acting like they think they're a lot older and that

10

we're like babies or something. They're only concerned about magazines and clothes and stuff like that. They don't seem to want to have anything to do with us."

"Then just ignore them," Maryann said. "Play hard to get. Stop acting like all you care about is whether they'll play with you. Play on your own, and make it look like fun."

"It *is* fun!"

"I know. So go ahead. They'll soon get bored with reading all week. And they'll get too hot to stay on the beach. It's nice and cool in the underbrush away from the beach, isn't it? Where the sun doesn't get through?"

Daniel nodded. "So Yo-Yo and I should just go off and do whatever we want? And try to make it look like fun, whether they want to join or not?"

"Exactly. And at lunch you can talk about the great time you had."

"Well, I'll give it a try."

"What're you going to do, Dan?"

"I don't know yet. Probably just hike and sneak around the dunes and the underbrush, just pretending."

"The twins may not think that's any fun," Maryann cautioned.

"They enjoyed it last year," Daniel said, shrugging.

"Yeah, but apparently they see themselves as much older and wiser now."

"I don't care. *We'll* have fun at least."

Daniel was on his way out when Theresa burst in the door, her dark hair flying.

"Is Yolanda here?" she shouted.

"No," Daniel said, "she's still at the beach."

"No, she's not! She's missing!"

The adults seemed to appear from nowhere. They asked questions all at the same time.

"I don't know. I don't know!" Theresa wailed. "We were reading. We saw Daniel leave. He said he was coming here. But a few minutes later we looked up and Yolanda was gone. We couldn't see her anywhere!"

"Had she gone into the water?" Mrs. Bradford asked quickly.

"I don't think so. I don't know. We weren't watching."

"We've got to get down there, Steve," Mr. Bradford said. "Jim, bring your scuba equipment." They hurried all about and then raced out the door.

"Where's Tom?" Theresa's mother demanded.

"He's still down there, checking the water." And Theresa burst into tears.

2

The Search Begins

The Bradfords and Hubers showed up at the shore within a minute of each other. Since Yolanda was nowhere in sight, Mr. Bradford asked if it would be all right if he assigned teams to go look for her.

"Of course," Mr. Huber said. "Just tell us what you want us to do. Did you want Jim to check the water with his gear?"

"I don't think so, Steve. Her robe is missing, too. And she wouldn't have worn that in the water. Tom, Theresa, you don't remember her wading in the robe, do you?"

They shook their heads.

Mr. Bradford looked into all the worried faces. "Let's split up into twos," he said. "I'll go with Jim. Lil, you go with Maryann. Steve, why don't you go with Tim? And Carolyn, you take Theresa."

"What about me?" Daniel asked.

"Oh, yeah. Uh, you pick whatever team you want to go with. But let's fan out and go in as many different directions as we can. Just keep calling Yolanda or Yo-Yo and ask anyone you see if they've seen her. Her robe is turquoise. Otherwise, she's in a yellow and red suit. We'll meet back at the cabin in an hour."

The pairs started out before Daniel had decided which team to go with. He was hurt that his father had forgotten him. It made him a little mad, too. Otherwise, he probably would have wanted to go with his father and Jim. Now he didn't.

If he didn't decide soon, he'd be left behind. For some reason, he ran to catch up with Mrs. Huber and Theresa. Neither of them appeared too alarmed. And they didn't seem to be in any hurry.

"What's your strategy?" Daniel asked, panting.

"What do you mean, our strategy?" Mrs. Huber said. "We're just going to look and call and hope your little sister didn't get too far, that's all."

"But aren't we going to ask anyone from other cabins if they saw her or anything?"

"Feel free."

She sounded cold, Daniel thought. He didn't know what to think about it. Mrs. Huber and her daughter moseyed along the paths between the cabins. Occasionally they called Yolanda's name. Daniel scurried about, calling for her and knocking on every door. No one had seen her.

The farther they went, the slower Mrs. Huber and Theresa walked and the less they called for her. Daniel was becoming frantic, nearly in tears.

"Oh, now, dear," Mrs. Huber said, "she couldn't have gotten this far already anyway. Your parents or one of the other teams have probably already found her."

Daniel had always liked Mrs. Huber. She was a pretty woman and seemed like a lot of fun. But now he was mad at her. He couldn't control himself. "You don't even care!" he shouted. "Just because she's not your daughter!"

Carolyn Huber looked stunned and was quiet for a minute. "We don't have to get angry about it," she said finally. "Don't blame me if your new little sister doesn't know enough to stay put on the beach."

"She could have been kidnapped!" Daniel yelled.

14

"Oh, I think Tom or Theresa would have noticed if someone had carted her off, Daniel."

Daniel shook his head. "You really *don't* care!"

Mrs. Huber shrugged. "I care, I guess. But I don't think a temporary disappearance is worth getting this upset about yet."

"When *will* it be worth it, then?"

"In twenty-four hours."

"Twenty-four hours!"

"That's what the police would do."

Daniel was puzzled. "What do you mean?"

"The police don't even file a missing person report until someone has been missing for twenty-four hours. Too many kids wind up sleeping at a friend's house or going into the city to watch a movie or something. So many wind up right under their parents' noses. The police have learned to wait and see. Seems that's usually the best policy."

"What if it was one of the twins?" Daniel felt mean and ornery and knew he shouldn't be talking to an adult that way, but he couldn't seem to help it.

"It wouldn't be one of the twins," she said with assurance.

"They've never been lost?"

"No."

"It could happen."

"I doubt it. They're very responsible."

"If Yolanda wasn't, we wouldn't be so worried about her. We'd just figure she had run off and got into mischief again. But that's not like her. She's usually really good about that."

"Well, this is an exception, I'd say."

Daniel stared at Mrs. Huber, trying to make sense out of what she was saying.

"An exception?"

Mrs. Huber seemed embarrassed and looked over Daniel's shoulder. "I would just say that, ah, confident, bright, responsible, young people of Yolanda's type are rare."

Suddenly it hit Daniel. She was trying to say that because Yolanda was Mexican, or adopted, or something, she was naturally not a responsible child.

The three stopped in the middle of the path. Mrs. Huber looked at her daughter, then at Daniel. "Tell me again how you came to take her in."

"It isn't like we took her in," Daniel said, feeling his face redden and his heart pound. "It wasn't pity or anything like that. We wanted somebody closer to my age. And she was just perfect."

"Perfect?"

"Yes!"

"If you say so. I should think it might have put unusual strain on the family."

"What do you mean? It's been great!"

"There haven't been any problems with the neighbors or schoolchildren? Nothing at all like that?"

"The neighbors love her!"

"And kids at school?"

"She has lots of friends. She's a super student. And that makes her a favorite of a lot of teachers."

"Indeed?" she said.

Daniel nodded.

Mrs. Huber looked genuinely surprised. "And do they take into consideration her background when they make assignments or evaluate her schoolwork?"

"Not that I know of."

They walked on, and Daniel kept checking his watch. He hoped and prayed that someone had already found Yolanda and that all his worrying would be for nothing. She had been the best thing that ever happened to him. He couldn't imagine his life without her. He didn't even want to think about it.

They got along so well and had grown to really love each other so much. Daniel just knew they would be close friends all their lives. He kept praying silently that she would be all right. And that even if she was lost or had been found by a stranger, Yolanda wouldn't be too terribly scared.

"There haven't been *any* problems?" Mrs. Huber tried. "I mean with having someone of a different color or, uh, a different race in the home?"

"Course not. What kind of trouble could there be?"

"Kids calling her names."

"Oh, sure. We've had that. But we don't care. It bothers Yolanda some. But Mom and Dad have taught her that the ones with real problems are the ones calling the names. Yolanda is no different than us except that she's darker skinned and has a different background. It's no big deal."

"I mean those are big differences. She's not an American, she's no—"

"She is *too*!"

"Excuse me, Daniel. I'm talking. She at least wasn't born here. She's of a different culture. She'll have different interests and values. It'll only get more difficult as she gets older."

"It hasn't been difficult!"

"Not difficult? What do you call this mess? She's probably trying to find her way back to Mexico right now."

3

Reporting Back

Mrs. Huber had been correct. Even in the small resort town, the police refused to become involved until the person had been missing at least twenty-four hours.

Mr. Bradford was more than frustrated. He was angry. Mrs. Bradford was already crying.

"So nobody turned up anything?" Daniel asked when they were all back together.

"That's right," his mother said, fighting to stay calm. "What are we going to do?"

"Mom!" Maryann called from the bedroom she shared with Yolanda. "More of Yo-Yo's clothes are missing! She's been here!"

"While we were out looking for her, you mean?" Mr. Bradford said.

"I don't know. I didn't check to see if any of her clothes were gone before we went looking for her."

"Then she's gone on purpose?" Mrs. Bradford said. "What possibly could have caused that?" She looked at Tom and Theresa who seemed to be ignoring her. "What happened on the beach this morning?" she demanded.

They both shrugged. "We were reading," Tom said.

"You noticed that Daniel was gone, didn't you?"

"Yeah. Eventually."

"But you didn't notice anything else? She didn't seem upset? She wasn't arguing with anyone, either you two or Daniel?"

"She wasn't angry with me!" Daniel insisted. "In fact, we were having a great time. We just wanted Tom and Theresa to play with us, that's all."

"So you were arguing about that?"

"No. I just asked them what they wanted to do. Yolanda didn't have anything to do with it. They never talked to her."

"That's right," Theresa said. "We didn't talk to her at all."

Mrs. Bradford asked, "Why didn't you?"

Mrs. Huber came to her children's defense. "Now Lillian, don't be blaming my kids just because yours ran off."

"She wouldn't run off without a reason, Carolyn! Something must have happened down there."

"Well, nothing did. You just heard that for yourself. Who knows why a child like Yolanda would do what she does?"

"What do you mean?"

"I'm just saying that children are hard to understand sometimes, that's all."

"I know what she means," Daniel said. "She thinks we shouldn't have even adopted Yolanda."

"I didn't say that. I—"

"You think she's been nothing but trouble, and that it was too much of a strain on our family to adopt a Mexican."

"Carolyn!" Mrs. Bradford said. "You don't really, do you?"

Mrs. Huber looked embarrassed, but also angry. "Well, I would say this is a strain, wouldn't you?"

"But Carolyn! Yolanda has been one of the best things that ever happened to our family! You don't think—"

Mr. Bradford interrupted. "This is not helping us find Yo-Yo," he said. "We can discuss this later."

"We should discuss it right now," Mrs. Bradford said.

19

"Because if this is the way Carolyn feels, then it may be the way her children feel. And something of that attitude may have come through to Yo-Yo."

"If you people love this girl so much," Steve Huber said, "why do you keep calling her a yo-yo?"

"It's her nickname," Jim explained. "She got it from the other kids in the children's home. It comes from the first syllable of her first name and the last syllable of her last name. Her last name used to be Trevino."

Mr. Huber nodded.

"Apparently, you agree with your wife," Mr. Bradford said.

Steve looked away. "Well, like you say we can have this discussion anytime. The important thing now is to find the girl and make sure she doesn't find her way back to her own people. Or even start heading toward Mexico."

"I don't believe this!" Maryann shouted. "Mom! Dad! I thought these people were your Christian friends!"

"They are," Mr. Bradford said. "And we're going to have to find some time to talk this out. But first we've got to find Yolanda. Anyone who's interested and who cares can come with me. Otherwise, stay here and wait for us."

"I'm sure she'll turn up," Mrs. Huber said. "We'd probably just be in the way."

Mrs. Bradford glared at her. Then she stormed out to the driveway where the rest of the family met her a minute later.

"Until twenty-four hours have passed since she disappeared," Mr. Bradford said, "we're in this alone. Apparently the Hubers aren't that concerned. So we'll have to find Yolanda ourselves. I'm praying she wasn't kidnapped. Because sometimes kids disappear these days and never turn up."

The Hubers emerged from the cottage with their swimming gear. As they headed toward the beach, Mrs. Huber called out, "Good luck."

"I don't care if we ever see them again," Maryann said. "I don't care. I had no idea how horrible they were."

"They're not horrible," her father said. "They are wrong.

20

And they seem to be blind to their own prejudice. But there are a lot of wonderful things about the Hubers. They're usually kind and generous, they're—"

"Please!" Mrs. Bradford said. "Let's just find Yolanda!"

Mr. Bradford sent Daniel with his brother and sister to the little business district where people bought supplies, bait, and food. There were several little shops and a couple of restaurants. But no one had seen Yolanda or anyone suspicious.

Daniel was getting scared. He wished he could just cry. But he didn't want to do that in front of Jim and Maryann. "What do you think of the Hubers now?" he asked.

"You don't want to know," Maryann said. "But I wondered about them from the beginning this time. Mom and Dad had trouble finding a week that was convenient for them to join us. But nobody thought anything about it at the time. Then, when they finally did get together on the right dates, the Hubers didn't seem that enthusiastic."

"Yeah, I know," Jim said. "Remember how many cards and letters we got after we sent the Christmas cards with the news about Yolanda joining our family? The Hubers sent us a card and didn't mention Yolanda. In fact, it was addressed to Mr. and Mrs. Bradford, Jim, Maryann, and Daniel."

"You're kidding."

"No, don't you remember? Mom thought they must not have gotten our card. So she sent another and a special letter. But they never answered."

Daniel nodded. "They didn't seem real thrilled to meet Yolanda."

"I didn't notice that," Jim said. "Except that the twins didn't seem happy to come this year."

"I thought that was just because they were jerks," Daniel said.

Maryann almost laughed. "They're nothing to write home about, are they?"

"What're we going to do now, Jim?" Daniel asked.

"We're not giving up, I'll tell you that." He led the way

to the bait shop at the edge of the water on the way out of town.

"What would make the Hubers so prejudiced?" Maryann asked.

"What's that mean?" Daniel asked.

"It means that someone had judged somebody else in advance."

"In advance of what?"

"In advance of everything. Before they even get to know the person, they prejudge him for some other reason."

"Like his race or color of skin," Maryann said.

"So, even without knowing Yolanda, they have decided there's something wrong with her?" Daniel asked.

Maryann nodded. "Only they can't even say what it is. They think she would be happier with her own kind of people—whatever that means."

"Or even that she would want to go back to Mexico," Daniel added.

"Yeah," Jim snorted. "As if she would remember what that was like after not having been there since she was a baby."

"The Hubers even think she's caused problems for our family," Daniel said.

Jim paused in front of the screen door of the bait shop. The smell of fish was heavy, but Daniel liked it. A stiff wind increased the waves. The sky was clouding over.

"Problems for our family," Jim said slowly as if he was turning it over in his mind. "Whatever problems we might have had were solved when Yolanda joined us. As I recall, we had an obnoxious little brother who was always in the way because he didn't have anyone to play with."

Jim winked at Daniel and held the door open for him and Maryann. He let it slam. The spring twanged as it settled back into place.

The place was empty except for the owner. He shuffled out from the back room. He was a wide, old man, and he wore a white and blue striped train engineer's cap. "My

22

goodness, city folk!" he said. "From the slammin' of the door which I 'preciate, I'da guessed it was locals. They know the slam is what tells me someone's here. Most city folk are so polite they shut the door nice an' easy. And then they don't think nobody's here 'cause I'm in the back makin' lures. So, what kin I do fer ya?"

"We're looking for our little sister," Jim said. "Been missing more that an hour from down at the beach. Turquoise robe or yellow and red suit. Nine years old. But a little small for her age."

The old man thought for a while and then said, "Nope, not if she looks like you folk. Only little girl in here alone this mornin' was wearin' jeans and a navy blouse, more like a denim shirt. Carryin' a bag, one of them little canvas jobs. But she wouldn't belong to you. She was a Mexican."

4

At Last Some Breaks

"That's her!" Jim shouted. And he showed the man a photograph of Yolanda.

"Sure enough," the man said. "But I thought you said she was your sister."

"Adopted," Maryann said.

"Ah," the old man said, nodding. "I was 'dopted myself. Well, lemme see if I can help you find her. Was she unhappy about anything?"

"Not that we know of. But something might have happened on the beach with some friends this morning. We just don't know."

"Well, she looked like she'd been cryin' when she came in here."

"What did she want?" Jim asked. "I mean, did she buy anything?"

"Uh, yeah, let me think. She bought a postcard and a stamp and asked me where was a mailbox. I told her up the hill, that way."

"And did she head that way?"

"Yup. Bought herself some snacks too. Couple dollars

24

worth is all. Didn't start eatin' 'em right away like most kids do. Stuffed 'em in her bag."

"What time was she here?"

"Maybe forty-five minutes ago."

"You sure?"

"Not really. Important?"

"Well, we're just trying to figure out if she came straight here from the beach. Or if she went to our cottage first."

"She must have come from the cottage," Daniel said. "Because I don't remember her having that bag. All she had was a towel. And she was wearing her thongs."

"This girl wasn't wearin' no thongs," the man said. "She had shoes on, you know, track shoes, runnin' shoes."

"Anything else?" Jim asked.

"Not that I can think of. Sure hope you find her real quick. Storm's comin'."

Jim thanked the man and hurried out. Maryann and Daniel followed him as he jogged up the hill toward the mailbox. He read the card that said the morning mail had been picked up about twenty minutes before.

"Wonder who picked it up?" he thought aloud.

"Probably the mailman while he was on his route. Then he takes it back to the post office to be sorted before delivering it tomorrow."

Jim began asking peole if they had seen the mailman and which direction he usually went. He finally found him six blocks north and three blocks west. He was a young, friendly, sandy-haired man in shorts and a pith helmet.

"Did you pick up the mail in that box yet?"

"Yeah," the mailman said, smiling. "And I wish I hadn't. Didn't realize how heavy it was. Now I have to lug it all the way around the rest of my route before getting it back to the post office."

Jim hurriedly told him their story. He asked if they could look through the mail for Yolanda's postcard. The man hesitated. "I guess that would be all right," he said finally. "I can't let you keep it unless it's addressed to you. But if it's a

25

postcard, you can read it. And we have to hurry. I don't have a lot of time."

The problem was that there were dozens of postcards. It seemed everyone on the shore that week wanted to brag about it to friends and family back home.

"Turn them all over," Daniel said. "I'll recognize her handwriting right away."

With all the cards face down on the ground, Daniel soon spotted Yolanda's.

"Here it is," he said.

It was addressed to "Mr. and Mrs. Bradford, Shore Cottage."

"Do you know," the mailman said, "that this card never would have been delivered? There's not enough address. And for a postcard, we don't spend any time trying to figure out which visitor it might belong to."

Jim shook his head and read the card aloud. "She must've thought it would be delivered today, too. It says, 'Dear Mom and Dad, Don't worry about me. I'm going to use my allowance to get a boat and row to the island. I'll be back after supper. The twins hate me. Love, Yolanda.'"

"The island?" Maryann shouted. "Not that little—"

"Yes," Jim said. "The one we showed her when we were on the beach last night."

"But we've never been out there by ourselves!" Maryann said. "All we told her was that Mom and Dad took us out there when Daniel was real little."

"I remember it," Daniel said. "But not very well. It was hot and dry and sandy, that's all I know. And Jim and Dad dragged me out to go fishing while Mom and Maryann were lying on the beach."

"That's about all the little island is good for," Maryann said. "There's nothing to buy, nothing to eat or drink, no buildings, no nothing. All you can do is swim, sunbathe, and fish."

"Good fishing, though," Jim said. "Anyway, they won't let Yolanda row out there by herself. It's more than a half mile. And I don't think she even knows how to row. There's got to be some kind of age or size limit. I hope when she found out she couldn't go, she just went back to the cottage."

"Is anyone there?" Maryann asked. "Mom and Dad are out looking on the other end of the shore. And the Hubers are at the beach."

"Don't mention the Hubers to me," Jim said. "I don't even want to think about them. The twins must have said or done something to Yolanda at the beach this morning. Otherwise, why would she have written that? Why would she want to spend the day at the island?"

"We can worry about that later," Maryann said. "Let's get over to the island boat launch."

The launch was run by two college kids, a boy and a girl. They were obviously more interested in each other than they were in the boats they were renting. "Row or motor?" the girl said lazily as Jim approached.

"I don't want a boat," he said. "I want to know if you saw this little girl around here this morning."

The girl took the photograph and showed it to her boyfriend. "Is this the girl you tried to talk out of rowing to the island?"

He studied it. "Yeah. I tried to talk her into a motorboat. It's only ten bucks. But she wanted to row."

Jim stared at him. "You tried to talk a nine-year-old girl into a motorboat?"

"Hey, don't jump on my case, man. She had plenty of money."

"And that's all that mattered, huh? Did you let her take a rowboat then?"

"Course. I had to show her how to handle it, though. She'd have been better off with a motor."

"Sure. Then what would she have done if the motor died? Paddle with her hands?"

"I could have sent some oars along."

"So, what's the story? She rented a rowboat and headed out to the island?"

27

"Yeah, and she was doin' pretty good, too. I taught her well."

"Yeah, I'll bet you did," Jim said. "You just better hope nothing happens to her."

"What's that supposed to mean, big shot?"

"You just better hope you don't have to find out. If I were you, I wouldn't rent a boat, row or motor, to any more kids. Somebody's going to get hurt or lost or drowned. And you'll be in big trouble."

Neither the boy or his girl friend had anything to say to that. So Jim asked to rent a motorboat. "That'll be twenty bucks. I'll give you ten of it back when you return the boat."

"Maryann, do you have any money?"

She checked her wallet. "About four dollars."

"Dan?"

"Just some change."

"I've only got a buck," Jim said. "How about letting me take it, and I'll bring you the money later."

"Oh, sure, you come along with the big lecture, and then you think I'm gonna feel bad enough to let you take a boat without paying for it. I'd be in real trouble with my boss then."

"Where's your boss?"

"Lives a couple of miles from here. But I never know when he's gonna show up. What if I let you out there in a motorboat, and he comes by to take the money to the bank? I won't have enough for the boats that are out. Then Trixie and me get ourselves fired."

Jim explained why it was an emergency.

"I don't care if the island blows up with your little sister on it. You're not going to be there to see it unless you come up with the twenty bucks."

Jim kept his temper and gritted his teeth. "There's some money in the cottage," he told Maryann. "I'll go get it."

"I'll try to find Mom and Dad," she said. "They should know where Yolanda is and quit worrying."

"Good idea. Dan, wait for us here. We'll be right back."

Jim and Maryann went jogging off in different directions.

Daniel he knew he was supposed to love his enemy and pray for people who used him badly. This guy had certainly used Yolanda badly. The sky grew darker and the wind blew colder, even at the time of day when the sun was supposed to be highest in the sky. Daniel walked up and down the pier. He prayed that he would have the right attitude toward the guy who rented Yolanda a boat.

But he felt so angry and disgusted with the boy that he knew he couldn't change his mind about him. Only God could do that. So he prayed even harder.

5

The Boat

Daniel waited about ten minutes. Then he started getting antsy. He wondered if Jim was able to get back into the cabin. He wondered whether the Hubers were there. He wondered if Jim had gotten into an argument with them.

He wondered if Yolanda was all right. He wondered if Maryann had found their parents. He wondered whether they would be coming. He knew he shouldn't worry and wonder so much. But there was little else to do.

He wished he'd thought to bring his windbreaker. It was getting cold. And not only was the sky cloudy, but it was so overcast that he couldn't make out a single cloud. The entire sky was dark. The pennants hanging from the ropes along the piers—not to mention the sign advertising boats for rent—were standing straight in the stiff wind.

Daniel searched the horizon. There were no boats on the water now. He could see the island in the distance. He didn't see any boats near the island either. But he decided he was too far away to be able to tell for sure.

He looked back toward the road. He didn't see Jim or Maryann or his parents or anyone. A couple of cars drove past, along with a pickup truck. But the swimmers and boaters and fishermen were nowhere in sight. They were all inside, certain that the weather was going to be as nasty as the skies promised.

The young man and woman began to tidy up the boat rental area. It was clear that only one boat remained out on the water—the rowboat that Yolanda had rented. *And this creep taught her to row it,* Daniel thought.

"Hope you're happy now!" he heard himself say.

"What's that?" the boy said. His girl friend laughed.

"I said I'll bet you're glad you gave my little sister such good boating lessons now that she's going to be out in a storm on her first day of rowing."

"I don't see her anywhere," the boy said. "She probably is safe and sound on the island. And will still be there when the storm is over. Don't worry about her."

"That's easy for you to say," Daniel said. But the boy wasn't listening. He was watching a late model, green sedan pull off the road and down toward the pier. A middle-aged man in slacks, a sports coat, and an open-neck shirt got out of the car.

"Everything going OK, Eddie?" the man said.

"Yes, Mr. Connors," the young man said. "One boat's still out but it's on the island."

The man rubbed his palm across his face and stared out over the water. "Don't be renting any more boats until the sun is shining and it's quit raining for a half hour."

"That might not be until tomorrow," Eddie said.

"Maybe so," Mr. Connors said. He noticed Daniel. "Better beat it, kid. We're not renting any more boats until late this afternoon or tomorrow."

Daniel wanted to tell him about his sister. He wanted to tell him that his brother was hurrying back with some money to rent a boat so they could find her. But he didn't know how to begin or what to say.

Mr. Connors turned back to Eddie and Trixie. "Padlock those motorboats and tie up the others. Be sure and come back if the storm quits, hear?"

"Yes, sir. And here's today's receipts so far."

Daniel moved to the end of the dock and sat down. He hoped they wouldn't notice him. But Mr. Connors passed him on the way to his car.

"Better get home, kid. Storm's coming, and your mom'll be worried about you."

Daniel nodded. He watched as the big car swung back out onto the road. Something caught his eye as he looked for Jim down the hill. Someone was walking toward him. Whoever it was didn't seem to be in a hurry. He was just walking and looking around.

As he drew closer, it was clear the walker was a young, dark-haired boy. And he was calling for someone. Finally Daniel knew who it was. It was Tom Huber, and he was calling for Yolanda! It didn't make sense.

Eddie and Trixie finished securing the boats and left the pier. They reminded Daniel to get out of there as they went by.

He started off toward Tom. That apparently made the couple think he was leaving. Eddie was lugging a heavy metal can.

"Get all the gas drained?" Trixie asked.

He grunted and nodded as he heaved the can on the back of his pickup.

Daniel ran to Tom. "Tommy!" he called. "What're you doing here?"

"Looking for your sister, what else?"

"Still? I thought your family wasn't interested and that you were at the beach."

Tom shrugged. "I kept checking back at the cabin to see if you or someone had found her. But no one had. So I told my parents I was going to go exploring. I've been looking for her ever since. Have you guys had any luck?"

Daniel told him the whole story. Tom stood there shaking his head the whole time, looking miserable. "So, what did you and your sister do or say to her this morning when I was gone?"

"It was me, Daniel. My sister felt the same way. But she

32

didn't really do or say anything. I sneaked up behind Yolanda and pushed her down. Then I kicked sand on her and splashed her with water from her bucket."

"Why?"

"I don't know. I just felt like it. I called her names, too."

"Like what?"

"Oh, you know, like Mex and—stuff like that."

"Why, Tom? Why would you do that? What did she ever do to you?"

"Nothing. But you know how Mexicans are. We used to live near some and they were lazy, out of work, always drinking and everything."

"Hey, we live near white Americans who are just like that, Tom. It doesn't have anything to do with whether someone's Mexican or not."

Tom shrugged.

"Why did you change your mind about looking for her?" Daniel asked.

"Well, to tell you the truth, I started feeling guilty. I had fun with you last year. I knew you were a good guy and everything. But I couldn't figure out how you could stand having a foreigner in your family. But then when she ran off like that, I knew it was my fault. I didn't really mean any harm. I'd hate for her to be lost or have anything happen to her, especially in this storm."

"Well, we're not going to find her around here. She's out on the island. At least she was headed that way. They've shut down the boat rental. So I don't know what Jim or my parents are going to do when they get back here."

"Maybe they've already figured they can't go out in this weather. Maybe they're just going to wait it out," Tom suggested.

Daniel looked around. "Maybe. Because at least one of them should have been back by now."

Tom ran toward the boat dock.

"Where're you going?" Daniel called after him, trying to catch up.

"To see how secure these boats are. Maybe we could borrow a motorboat real quick. We could get out to the island before the storm starts."

"The motorboats are drained of gas," Daniel said. "I saw the guy do it myself. Anyway, they're padlocked. Besides that, it would be illegal."

"Not in an emergency," Tom said. "Who would get a kid in trouble for trying to save someone's life?"

Daniel followed him down the pier to the rowboats. Each had its oars attached. Tom dug in his pocket for a knife.

"You don't have to cut the rope!" Daniel yelled. "It's just tied in a knot. Anyway, you don't want to cut all the boats loose, do you? We could never explain that."

Daniel lay on the pier on his stomach. He reached for the knot. He quickly untied it. He waited until Tom had removed one small rowboat, then tied the knot again. "You want to row first or you want me to?" Tom asked.

Daniel stepped carefully into the boat and almost capsized it. "I'll start," he said. He sat on the middle seat. Grabbing the oars, he tried to maneuver the boat out into the water toward the island. He was so eager to get going that he knew he would have to do something more than just sit and watch Tom row.

"Looks like I'd better do it," Tom said.

"Why?"

"Because you've got the flat end of the boat facing the direction you want to go. Look at the other end." The other end, facing the shore, was pointed. "See. That end's made for heading into the water. Here, let me turn it around."

Tom turned the boat around quickly, showing that he had plenty of experience. When it was pointed directly toward the island, he looked carefully over his shoulder. He began rowing with long, steady pulls on the oars. The boat glided straight and smooth through the waves, which were getting higher every minute.

Daniel envied Tom's skill with the boat. He watched him so he'd know what to do when it was his turn. From far in

34

the distance, he heard the first low rolls of thunder. "We don't want to be out here when the lightning starts!" he called.

"Better pray there's *no* lightning!" Tom said. "It always strikes the highest object. And out in the middle of the ocean, you know what that'll be!"

Daniel knew there would be lightning eventually. The thunder proved it. But he prayed against it anyway. And while he was at it, he prayed for Yolanda. She just had to be on the island. Because if she wasn't, who knew where her little boat might have drifted? If it was out in the middle of nowhere when the storm hit, she'd never survive.

6

The Storm

Daniel sat with his back to the shore, facing Tom, who was rowing for all he was worth. "Keep me on course!" the older boy yelled.

"How?" Daniel could hardly hear himself over the sound of the waves and the wind.

"I should be lined up right between you and the island!" Tom shouted. "If I start straying off course, just signal to me to change."

Daniel sat right in the middle of the seat board. He stared ahead at the island. The island came into full view, not blocked by Tom's hardworking body. Daniel waved him to the left. Tom let up a little with his right oar and drove hard with the left. Daniel signaled him that he was straight again.

Tom was huffing and puffing. The strong current was pushing him back toward the shore. To Daniel it seemed they were making hardly any progress at all. A big wave rocked them until the bow was pointing toward the sky. They charged back on the other side, and he wondered if the island would still be in sight when they were level again.

There wasn't even a hint of the sun—just rather that

scary, greenish sky that always comes before the worst rain-storms. Daniel was cold. He wished he had a jacket, a blanket, anything. And he hoped Yo-Yo had thought to take along something warm.

The thunderclaps were closer and louder and longer now. But still Daniel hadn't seen any lightning. He decided that was a good sign. Tom looked tired. His strokes on the oars were shorter. The boat was angling side to side. It seemed all Daniel was doing was signaling him to stay on course. "You can do it, Tom! Keep pushing! Keep pushing!"

It took nearly half an hour to get about a quarter of a mile from the shore. They were about midway between the pier and the island. The darker it grew, the less Daniel could keep them on course. By now he was sure there were no boats on the side of the island he could see. Anyone who was still there was either docked on the other side or had carried his craft ashore.

Tom's feet were sliding along the wet bottom of the boat with each pull now. The boat was going nowhere. It was clear he was exhausted.

"Want me to take over?" Daniel asked. He was not sure he could do any better, even though he would be fresher.

Tom shook his head and kept struggling. But finally his arms fell limp, and the oars banged against the side of the boat. One began to slip through its metal ring, and Daniel lurched to keep it from sliding away.

"Switch places!" Daniel screamed. He stood with his legs spread far apart, leaning over his weak companion. It was all Tom could do to let himself fall from his seat. But that made the boat tip, and Daniel fought to regain his balance.

He twisted around and slammed to a sitting position where Tom had been. The oars felt cold and slippery. Tom crawled to where Daniel had been and sat down. But by the time Daniel had the oars even and level, the boat had turned sideways against the waves.

"Oars up!" Tom screeched.

Daniel didn't even know what he meant.

"Oars up!" he repeated, and Daniel instinctively pushed down with his hands to lift the other ends of the oars out of the water. He had caught on just in time. A huge wave, crashed over the boat, sending it careening back toward the shore.

"If you'd had the oars in the water, we'd have gone over!" Tom yelled.

"Should we go back?" Daniel said. He was afraid that the next wave would capsize them.

"Not yet! Let's keep trying! If we can get near the island when the storm hits, we'll be blown that way and not this way! Put the right oar in the water. Steer us back on course! When you're straight, I'll tell you. Then you can start rowing with both."

The boat felt like a toy to Daniel. The ugly, deep green waves played with it. After he made several tries with the right oar, the boat seemed to somehow straighten itself out.

"There!" Tom called. "Now row with both, hard and fast!"

Daniel planted his feet, hunched his shoulders, and dropped both oars into the water. He tugged as hard as he could. The effort pulled him up off the seat and nearly bent him over backward. But there was progress! He felt movement! He knew the boat was going the way he wanted it to, at least for now.

That feeling gave him more strength. But he was still terrified of the dark sky and the huge waves and the icy winds. He wondered whether he would ever be on dry land again. Wherever Yolanda was, she had to be safer than this. And wherever his brother and sister and parents were, he wondered if they had any idea where he was.

Suddenly Tom yelled again, "Oars up!" Daniel didn't know why. The boat was straight, not turned. And he couldn't make his hands and arms react fast enough anyway. A huge wave broke over the front of the boat, filling it behind Daniel as the bow drove beneath the water.

The water gushed up over Daniel's back. It ran over the

top of his head down his face. He was freezing. "How would getting the oars out of the water have helped us there?" he yelled. Tom dropped to all fours and began splashing water out of the boat. They were riding perilously low in the ocean.

"I don't know!" Tom said. "But I saw it coming and figured we had to try something! Here comes another!"

This time Daniel forced the oars out of the water. But the water grabbed the right one and tore it from his hand. It caught Tom in the shoulder and blasted him off his feet toward the back of the boat. If his heel hadn't caught on the seat board, he'd have been thrown into the ocean.

The oar lazily swung back around toward Daniel. He reached for it even as it slipped away from him. The boat lurched. The oar slid further through its ring. Both boys reached for it as it disappeared.

Daniel slumped back to his seat, but Tom screamed. "We have to have that oar!" He grabbed the other oar and tried to paddle in a circle. But the lost oar bobbed and floated and darted through the waves, impossible to catch.

"What are we gonna do with one oar?" Daniel asked.

"Let's try this," Tom said. He carefully put the remaining oar through its ring and signaled Daniel to sit down and man it. "Use both hands!" he said.

"We'll go in a circle!"

"No we won't! Just row!"

Daniel followed orders and grabbed the oar. But the boat was so wet and slippery, he couldn't get any footing.

"Here!" Tom yelled. "Press your feet against mine!"

Tom was facing Daniel again. But now he was leaning over the other side of the boat. One arm was completely submerged in the water. "You row and I'll steer."

Daniel didn't know how long Tom could keep that up. But just seeing the exhausted boy working so hard—offering his feet as a brace for Daniel's own and leaning out of the boat to act as a rudder against the great storm—gave Daniel an extra surge of strength.

And then the rain started. It was a cold, stinging rain.

Daniel had to blink and squint to see Tom. For ten minutes, Daniel pushed and pulled and panted as he fought to make some headway against the storm. He finally dared peek over his shoulder. He found that he had indeed got them somewhat closer to the island.

Within a few more minutes, the waves were behind them instead of in front of them. Now they were hurtling toward the island faster than they could control the boat. Daniel could finally relax and rest his aching, knotted shoulder and arm muscles. He slumped in his seat. Tom screamed, but Daniel couldn't hear him.

He saw the older boy's mouth moving, and his face twisted. But Daniel couldn't react. He let go of the only remaining oar. As his horrified companion's eyes grew large with disbelief, it too slipped away. Tom nearly went over the side to get it. But Daniel pulled him back.

Daniel was aware of lightning for the first time. It seemed to be coming from the shore, and the deafening thunderclap nearly made him cover his ears. It was close. Too close. Much closer, and they would have been dead.

He tried to dredge up from his mind every Scripture verse he had ever memorized. He prayed and prayed, not even caring that Tom might hear him. "God, help us!" he cried. "God, help us!"

As another wave came hurtling down on them, it brought the oar with it. Daniel thought about reaching out for it as an answer to his prayer. But the oar blasted against the craft, leaving a gaping hole in the side.

Water filled the boat. Lightning flashed, and thunder roared. The waves tossed the craft around, driving it toward the island. Tom and Daniel fought to hang on. They slid from their seats and crashed into each other. They held onto each other's arms until they were torn apart. Then they grabbed the edge of the fast sinking boat.

Suddenly, the sky was a black as night. Daniel could feel Tom sliding past him. But he couldn't see him. He wouldn't have been able to see his hand in front of his face.

The rain tumbled over them in huge drops. They could hear the boat breaking up over the sounds of the rain, the wind, the waves, and the thunder. Lightning was flashing all around them. Daniel was pleading for God to spare their lives.

He was certain he was going to die. And he wondered what heaven would be like. He felt a strange sense of peace in knowing that he was a Christian, that he knew God, and that he would be safe in just a few minutes.

He wished there were some light. When the largest wave of the storm picked up what was left of the boat, the feeling he got was unlike anything he had ever experienced at an amusement park. The water lifted the boat and the boys forty feet straight up. Then it tumbled over them, smashing the boat to bits.

7

The Island

Daniel heard Tom wailing before he went under the water. Then there was silence. Utter silence. The only thing Daniel was aware of was water all around him. He was under the giant wave and felt himself pulled along.

He moved his arms to try to swim to the surface. But he realized he was so deep and there was such force and power under the tons of water that nothing he could do would have any effect. He was going to have to simply ride out the wave for as long as he could. He'd have to do everything possible to keep from swallowing any water.

If only he'd had some warning, some inkling that he was going to be under water for several seconds. Then he would have gulped as much air as possible. But already his lungs were bursting for want of oxygen. He knew if he allowed his mouth to fall open, he would take in enough water to kill himself.

God, give me strength! he prayed silently. *Let me hang on!* He felt himself flipping over and over under the torrent. He wondered if he would crash against something that would instantly end his life.

Suddenly Daniel felt himself pass through what felt like an undertow. And then it was as if he were floating down to a standing position. His feet hit something solid, his knees bent, and he realized he was standing on the bottom!

Nearly in a panic, he fought to keep his mouth shut and his breathing mechanism from gulping water. Was he way out from the island? Had the storm pushed him to the deep, deep bottom? Or was he closer to the shore, and was he standing in shallow water?

His eyes were open, but it was blacker underwater than it had been before. He knew his only chance to survive was to reach the top somehow. With adrenalin surging through his body, Daniel bent even lower and pushed off the bottom with all the force he could gather.

He reached high above his head so that he would know the moment he broke through. He prayed that no other wave would come crashing down on him before he was able to get some air.

Suddenly he broke through the surface. He nearly cried as he gasped for breath. It felt so rich and deep and good. Strength returned to him. He looked all about. He could make out shadowy forms and realized he was near the island and should be in fairly shallow water. But it was still nearly impossible to get his bearings.

He dog-paddled to stay above the surging sea. The next time a wave pitched him to the bottom, he kept his head above water and found himself standing in water up to his chest. He looked all around. "Hey!" he cried. "Hey, Tom! Are you there?"

He heard nothing.

Half running, half swimming he charged toward the shore. The rain was still heavy and stinging. The lightning was closer than ever. The thunder rattled his head from his shoulders. He was freezing in the inky darkness. Yet he knew it was only early afternoon on a summer day. Daniel was grateful to be alive.

He staggered and struggled until he could make out the

sandy shoreline. Several more halting steps and he was there. He threw himself to the sand and breathed deeply. He wished he could fall asleep forever and not have to move a muscle again.

Then another big wave covered him, and the undertow threatened to pull him back out to sea. Daniel stood and ran farther up onto the beach, safe from the waves and the lightning but not from the rain. He collapsed, wishing God would drop a fire and blankets from heaven to warm him.

Tom. Where was Tom? He wouldn't know where to start looking. But he knew he had to get up and out of the rain anyway. He lay face down with his head hidden in his arms for several minutes.

Finally, when a little strength seeped back to his muscles, he pulled himself nearly to his feet and crawled into the underbrush. Rain still dripped on him from the branches and bushes. But the wind wasn't so strong here.

Daniel drew up his knees and wrapped them in his arms. His whole body shook. He knew he needed to somehow get himself dried off. But there was no towel and not even an inch of his own clothing that wasn't drenched. Worse, he realized he had somehow lost a shoe.

As he sat there catching his breath, Daniel thanked God that he was alive, then started praying for Tom and Yolanda. He didn't know how long he sat there, breathing heavily. He couldn't shake the chill, and he hated the darkness.

"Daniel! Daniel!"

The call was coming from the water. It sounded like Tom. Daniel scrambled to his feet and fought his way out of the underbrush. If the rain had let up a little, he couldn't tell. The drops blinded him.

"Daniel! Daniel!" The voice was weaker now.

"Tom!"

"Over here!"

Daniel rubbed his eyes and scanned the shoreline. About twenty feet out, hanging onto a scrap of what was left of their boat, was Tom. He appeared too weak to swim to

44

shore. "You can walk from there!" Daniel called. "It's shallow."

"I'm afraid to let go! Too weak!"

"Get rid of the board. You can stand up there!"

Tom tried. Daniel saw the chunk of wood sweep past Tom and hurtle toward the shore. Tom went under and came up coughing and gasping. "Can't get my footing."

Daniel hurried out to him, hating to be back in the water. He didn't care if he was ever in this water again. Tom seemed to be lying face down on the water with his arms out to his sides. He didn't have enough strength left to fight anymore.

Daniel finally reached him. He flipped Tom over on his back and dragged him to shore by his chin. It was the way Daniel had been taught to do it. But he knew if he'd had to do it while swimming, he'd have failed.

He got Tom far enough onto the beach so that they were clear of the waves. They both collapsed in the sand. "There's a little shelter in the underbrush over there," Daniel managed finally to say, panting.

"Later," Tom said. And he lay still.

Daniel would have let him lie there for an hour if it hadn't been for the heavy rain. He knew it was ridiculous to think they could somehow dry off. But he decided it would be better for both of them if they didn't have to contend with the constant downpour of cold water.

The lightning began striking the island.

"We've got to get off the beach!" Daniel shouted. He helped Tom to his feet and half carried him into the underbrush.

"We also have to stay away from the trees," Tom said. "They'll act just like lightning rods in this weather."

For the next hour, the boys huddled in the cold, wet underbrush, shivering in the darkness. The lighting struck within a hundred yards of them. A giant tree lit up and split, forcing them to cover their ears against the almost simultaneous thunder.

"We have to find Yolanda," Daniel said when he finally felt he had regained some strength.

"There's no way we're going to find her until the sun breaks through again," Tom said. "Not unless she's right around here and she can hear us."

"She'd have to be only ten feet away to hear us in this storm," Daniel said.

"We're going to be sick if we don't get dry somehow," Tom said.

Daniel nodded. "I know. Maybe when the sun comes out we can dry out clothes on a rock and just hang around on the sand until we're warm and dry."

The rain stopped. Tom held out his hand, palm up, to see if any drops would hit it. None did. They could still hear some water dripping from the trees. But they knew the downpour was over, and that made them feel good.

"I'll bet there's no one else on this island," Tom said. "The weather report was bad all morning. Most everyone would know enough to head back to the mainland. Don't you think?"

"Yeah. Everybody but Yolanda. Unless someone noticed her and told her a big storm was coming, she probably stayed where she was."

"Is she that stupid?"

Daniel looked sharply at Tom. "She's not stupid at all. She's smart. But she's young. And she doesn't know anything about the weather or the ocean or even about how to row a boat, let alone in a storm. She's always concentrating real hard on one thing at a time. I'm guessing she started exploring or reading or something and didn't even notice that everyone else was leaving—fishermen, tourists, and all."

Tom shivered and shook his head.

"Hey," Daniel said, "you don't really think Yolanda is stupid, do you?"

Tom shrugged. "I don't know. No more stupid than any other Mexican, I guess."

"You really think Mexicans are dumber than other people?"

"Sure. They *are*. Don't you think so?"

Daniel shook his head.

"You don't? Really?"

"Course not. There's no proof of that. Where'd you ever get that idea?"

"I don't know. My parents, I guess."

"Man, Tom. We've got to talk about this sometime."

8

Looking for Yolanda

The cloud cover had thinned, and the wind had died down some. To Daniel, it seemed like dawn. He knew the sun was high in the sky somewhere. And he was glad the clouds weren't totally black as they had been.

The lightning and thunder subsided, and the temperature rose. The boys still shivered, however.

"Let's get out onto the beach so we'll catch the first warm rays," Tom suggested.

Daniel followed him out.

"Boy, am I sore," Daniel said, lowering himself carefully to the damp sand. "You?"

"Nah," Tom said. "I still have the chills, though."

Daniel wanted to start looking for Yolanda. "I think I'm going to start down this way," he said. "You want to go the other way and see who finds her first?"

Tom looked troubled. "I'd rather wait until we dry out, Dan. I really think we should. We're going to be real sick otherwise."

"I don't feel sick. Let's get going."

"Not me. I'm going to dry myself and my clothes as soon as the sun comes out."

"I am, too," Daniel said. "But meanwhile I'm going to get started. When the sun comes out, I'll stop and dry everything. But hanging around here now is just a waste of time."

"I thought you wanted to talk to me about your sister."

"I do, but that can wait. The important thing is finding her."

"I should tell you something, Daniel. Even though I felt guilty about what I said and did to her, and even though I hope she's all right, I still think I agree with my parents about the whole idea. She's different. She's not one of us, or one of you. She's going to mean nothing but trouble for you and your family. And this is an example."

"This doesn't have anything to *do* with her being Mexican, Tom! I've gotten in big trouble before myself! In fact, I ran away once and took Yolanda with me. That's probably why she thinks she can get away with it now."

"But she can't?"

"No way. My parents treat us all the same. She may have had a reason to be angry or upset. But there's no way she should have gone off on her own like this."

"Yeah! Well, I wouldn't want her in our family, I'll tell you that."

"You risked your life coming to this island to help find her, and you can say that?"

Tom shrugged. "If I had known the weather was going to be that bad, I wouldn't have come. And you wouldn't have, either."

"I sure would have. What was I supposed to do, leave her out here by herself? I admit the storm was bigger than I ever dreamed. But Yolanda was out here somewhere in it, too. I just hope she made it to the island. I don't think she would even have had the strength to get as far as we did without a boat."

The daylight was brighter, and Daniel could see that Tom was shaking. His teeth chattered, and his lips were blue. "I'm heading out, Tom. This island is only three miles around, so if we get started we can find her soon. If you see her or find her boat or anything—I figure it has to look just like the one we were in—give me a yell. Or keep coming around your way till you run into me. I'll do the same, OK?"

"I already told you, Bradford. I'm not going searching until I get dry and warm. If you want to go on, then go ahead. I'll run into you sooner or later."

Daniel was so mad he couldn't even answer. Instead he just turned away quickly. He stalked off, limping through the sand in one shoe and one sock.

"Hey, Bradford!" Tom called after him.

Daniel stopped but didn't turn around. "That your shoe? Washed up over there!"

Daniel turned to see where he was pointing. Sure enough it was. That would certainly make things easier. He pulled the shoe from the mucky sand and washed it out in the ocean.

He knew it wouldn't do him any good to wear a shoe like that. So he took off his other shoe and both socks, rinsed them all out, squeezed the excess water from them, and carried them with him as he started around the island. Daniel felt chilled to the bone.

As he moved around the bend, he stole a peek back at Tom. He was sitting in the sand, Indian style. Daniel couldn't tell from that far away, but Tom was probably still shivering. Just like Daniel was.

He wanted to hurry along and call for Yolanda. But there was still enough noise from the wind and waves that it would have been useless. The day was getting lighter by the minute, however, so he was able to search for her. He prayed she would be smart enough to stay near the edge of the underbrush so she could be seen.

He plodded along. His sore muscles and aching joints reminded him of the ordeal he had been through. He had read about such storms and people trapped in small boats. But he never dreamed he would experience one, let alone live through it. When Daniel thought of the different ways he could have been killed during the worst part of the storm, he shuddered. And prayed.

He hoped against hope that Yolanda had not had to go through the same thing.

Just before he went around to the side of the island, he looked toward the mainland. He wanted to see if his parents or Jim and Maryann were coming. He knew they would be worried about him, too. He just hoped they hadn't given up looking for Yolanda to look for him.

Strangely, even though the sun was finally starting to peek through the fast moving clouds above him, the mainland still looked dark. Apparently the storm was still at full strength there. He saw no craft on the water. No motorboats. No trawlers. Not even any Coast Guard cruisers or other emergency vessels that usually patrolled during such storms.

Lightning flashed near the mainland, and he wondered if even his family had not been allowed to venture out. It was clear the storm would not be back to the island. It was heading the other way. And the sun was toasty during the few times it was able to slide between the clouds.

Daniel wished the clouds would all move out. He wanted the sun to hang in a clear blue sky and start drying out everything on the island, starting with him.

He guessed he had walked almost a mile. He had tried to stay near the water where the sand was packed down and the walking was easier. And then he saw signs of a broken-up boat. He laid his socks and shoes across a big, black rock, and he ran back to the water's edge to investigate.

He wasn't ready to take off his shirt and pants yet. The wind would have been too cold on his bare skin. He felt cold and clammy and wished he could take a hot bath and sleep for a couple of days.

If only there were some fruit trees on the island, he thought. He hadn't eaten since breakfast, and his stomach was growling.

The pieces of wood in the sand looked old at first. But as

Daniel looked more closely, it was clear that they were fresh. They looked as if they could have come from the boat he and Tom had borrowed. And that gave him a bad feeling in the pit of his stomach.

There was no way that the wind and current could have pushed the fragments from their own boat all the way around to this part of the island. If this boat was just like theirs, it must have come from the same rental place. He looked for identifying marks but found nothing for certain.

Just then the sun came out hot and strong. Daniel had to squint because of the reflection off the sand. He quickly removed his shirt and pants and wrung them out as thoroughly as he could. He spread out the wrinkled clothes over the rock and lay in the sand in his underwear. In minutes, he felt warm and dry. The clothes would take longer. He slept.

It was a fitful sleep, full of strange and scary dreams. But every time Daniel felt he was going under the water or being torn apart by a gigantic wave, he stirred enough to remember where he was and that he had already survived the storm.

Occasionally he checked his clothes. He thought they were dry when they felt hot to the touch. But when he turned them over, he realized that the other side was still wet. He spread them out carefully again and lay down in the sand.

By the time he rose, it was midafternoon and he had a light sunburn that actually felt good. What didn't feel good was his hunger and thirst and the dryness of his lips and face. Still, there was no time to waste. Tom would probably already be half way around the island, maybe farther. Maybe he had already found Yolanda. Daniel could only hope so.

He dressed slowly. Everything was dry and salty except for his shoes, which were still a little soggy. He knew he'd get farther with them on, so he wore them anyway. Just before setting out again, he stared over at the mainland. Still dark. Still storming.

Daniel trudged on. He kept his eyes open for any signs of his sister or her boat. Or Tom. Or Jim, Maryann, or his parents. Several hundred yards up the shore, he saw half a white rowboat in pieces. He ran to it.

He fit together some boards that had a name wood-burned onto them, "Connors Boat Launch."

9

The Discovery

Daniel sank to his knees, sobbing. He knew there was no way Yolanda could have survived the storm the way he and Tom had. In fact, *they* almost hadn't. If Daniel hadn't had swimming lessons and Red Cross lifesaver training—and if Tom hadn't been a twelve-year-old athlete—neither of them would have made it to the shore alive.

Daniel prayed that somehow, some way, Yolanda had been saved. He didn't know how. He couldn't imagine how. But he prayed anyway. He didn't want to stand up again. He didn't want to go on. He didn't want to find her tiny, lifeless body washed up somewhere along the shore.

But he forced himself to keep moving. He walked on and on in spite of his tears and that terrible feeling that he had already lost her. *Why, oh why, did she have to go away?* Why had Tom Huber teased her and made fun of her? Why did Eddie at the boat launch have to be stupid enough to rent a rowboat to a little girl when bad weather was coming?

If anything had happened to Yolanda, Daniel knew it would be years before he would be able to forgive anyone who had anything to do with her death. Only God could forgive them.

He pushed on. Something made him call her name, and each time he said it, it bothered him more. He didn't know if he could stand much more. It seemed as if he were calling her back from the dead. "Yolanda! Yolanda! Yolanda!" he called. And then he would cry some more.

For another half an hour he worked his way around the island. He thought he was just about halfway. He should have run into Tom by now. Unless Tom had slept, too. Or found something. Or turned back. Daniel kept going. The sight of something in the distance seemed to draw him.

It was a post in shallow water, the kind that pilots tie their boats to. Of course there were no boats tied. But something was flapping in the breeze there. He decided to check it out, just to keep his mind working. If Yolanda were dead, he wasn't sure he wanted to live either.

When he finally got to the post, a line was still tied to it and a piece from the bow of a small boat was still there. Had the storm been so strong that it ripped a boat from its moorings? No one could have lived through a storm like that. It must have been worse on this side of the island than on the other.

By now all Daniel wanted to do was to get around to the other side again. He wanted to watch for his family, see if the storm was still hanging over the mainland, and find out what had happened to Tom. He was mad. Tom had come on this journey because he'd felt guilty about causing Yolanda to leave. Now he didn't even have the energy to stay with the rescue.

He headed off toward the other side with more speed and determination than he had before he'd found the pieces of Yolanda's boat. Suddenly, he heard a familiar voice.

"Daniel! Daniel Bradford, is that you?"

"Yolanda!" he screeched. "Where are you?"

"Up here. No, here. Look up. Now to your right! Hi! What are you doing here?"

She was waving to him from a tree. He nearly passed out from relief. "I was looking for you. Where have you— how did you—what did—I mean, Yo-Yo, what in the world happened?"

Daniel hurried into the underbrush and watched her climb down. He hugged her tight. He rummaged through her bag and gobbled a bunch of pretzels. Then he dragged her back out to the sand. "We've got to go find Tom. He came with me."

"I don't want to see Tom," she said. "You wouldn't believe what he did and said to me."

"Yes, I would. He told me. But, Yo-Yo, didn't the storm hit you?"

"Not until an hour after I got here. Boy, was it hard getting here! I almost turned back. By the time I got here, all the fishermen and everyone else were heading back. They warned me to go back. But by then I was so tired from rowing all the way here that I knew I'd have to rest first. I was too embarrassed to ask anyone to take me back. I mean, they'd have to tow my boat and everything."

"I'm sure someone would have done that for you," Daniel said.

"Well, I didn't want to ask. And, anyway, I thought the storm was just going to be some rain. One of the fishermen saw the weak little knot I tied in my rope. I saw him look all over for me and then tie it himself. He did a pretty good job. When the storm hit, the only thing that stayed was that knot he tied!"

Daniel told her the whole story, even up to the part about thinking she had been killed in the storm. She could hardly believe it. "You guys stole a boat?"

"We didn't steal it, Yo-Yo! It was an emergency. It's not as bad as you running off without telling anyone."

"I wrote and told them I would be back after dinner."

"If we hadn't found that postcard, they wouldn't have gotten it at all. You didn't have enough address on it. By the time you got back, we would have worried ourselves to death."

"I didn't want everyone to worry. I just had to get away. My family had been so nice to me that I can't stand it when other people are mean. You know, even Mr. and Mrs. Huber don't like me."

"How do you know that?"

"I could just tell. They didn't look at me when they talked to me. And they hardly talked to me at all. Only when Mom and Dad were around. And their kids hate me even more."

"But Tom feels bad, Yo-Yo. He risked his life coming over here."

"I wonder what made him change his mind. After what he said and did to me this morning, I would have thought he'd be thrilled if I got hurt or lost or even killed."

"Well, Yolanda, they're Christians. Even if the parents do have a bad attitude about you, it has to bother them now and then. I think Tom was real scared about your running off. And I know Theresa was. She was crying about it and everything."

"Really?"

"Yeah. Was she mean to you, too?"

"Not really. But she didn't help when Tom was bothering me. She just laughed right along with him."

"I don't know where he is," Daniel said. "We should have seen him by now. We're just a little way from where we landed. Maybe he started looking in the underbrush and got lost."

As they walked on, Yolanda was grinning.

"What's with you?"

"I was just thinking. I know I'm going to get in trouble for leaving and all that. But it's nice to know you care that much."

"We all did," Daniel said. "All of us. Jim and Maryann and Mom and Dad. Even Tom and Theresa."

Yolanda just shook her head and kept walking. "I'm so glad you're all right, Daniel. It's kind of funny, isn't it? You almost get yourself killed looking for me. And I wind up finding you instead."

"Funny isn't the right word for it, Yo-Yo, but it *is* strange."

The sun was high and hot now. The mainland came into view, and it was obvious the storm was still raging over there. Even now, no boats had ventured out into the ocean. Daniel began pointing out parts of the boat he and Tom had rowed.

"Wow," Yolanda said. "It's in pieces, just like mine. How are we supposed to pay for those?"

"That's the least of our trouble right now," Daniel said. And he began running.

"Where are you going?" she called after him, running to try to stay close.

"I see something up ahead!"

"What?"

"I don't know! But it's near where I left Tom! Come on."

She raced even faster. Daniel slowed a little, trying to catch his breath. He hadn't realized how much the storm had taken out of him until he tried to run after walking three miles in the sand looking for Yo-Yo.

Just about at the point where Daniel and Tom had parted, Daniel found Tom's shoes. No socks. Nothing else. Just his shoes. And marks in the sand where it looked like Tom had crawled.

Daniel followed the track around the bend. There he found Tom lying on his face in the sand about ten feet from the trees and underbrush. "Yolanda! Come quick."

He turned Tom over and noticed that his neck and hands were deep red from sunburn. His breathing was shallow and came in short gasps. He tried to open his eyes but couldn't. Daniel thought he heard a moan.

Tom was still shuddering, the way he had been when Daniel saw him last. He put the back of his hand against

Tom's forehead. It was hot as if sunburned, but it was white as if he had hidden it from the sun.

"Fever, Yo-Yo. And a bad one. He's really sick."

"What're we going to do, Daniel?"

"I don't know, Yolanda. I wish I did."

10

Help for Tom

"We studied about this at the end of the school year!" Yolanda said, wasting no time. "Are his clothes hot and dry?"

Daniel checked. "Yes! What is it?"

"It looks like sunstroke," she said. "He must have been exhausted from the storm. Then he fell asleep in the sun. You can see he tried to get to the shade but never did. We've got to get him under the trees."

She helped Daniel drag Tom into the shade. Then she felt his arm and face.

"He's not sweating, Daniel. That's bad. His skin is hot and dry. We need lots of cold water."

"All we have to carry it in is your canvas bag," Daniel said.

"What else do I have in there?"

Daniel looked. "Just a can of orange juice and your swimming stuff."

"A towel?"

"Yes, the big beach towel."

"Dump all that stuff out of there, Daniel. I can soak the towel in the ocean. I'll try to get as much water in the bag as

I can. You get his clothes off. When I get back, I'll just toss the towel over the bushes here and you can spread it over him. Then I can keep dumping water on him as long as I have the strength to keep running to the water. While I'm doing that you can rub his legs upward toward his heart."

"Right!"

Daniel struggled with the older boy's clothes. Yolanda ran to the water's edge with the towel and the empty bag. When she returned, she rolled her thongs up in a smaller towel and tossed the makeshift pillow over the bushes to Daniel. Then came the soggy beach towel.

Daniel carefully spread it over Tom. He stirred a little. "You can come in now, Yo-Yo," Daniel told her. He set to work rubbing Tom's legs.

"Feel dizzy," Tom moaned.

Yolanda raised his head so that he could sip some orange juice. "What's that noise?" he asked.

Neither Daniel nor Yolanda had noticed. It sounded like a low-flying plane. Maybe a helicopter. "Better check, Yo-Yo!" Daniel said.

She scurried out into the open. But the chopper was just moving out of sight over the tree line. She jumped and screamed. But there was no hint that she'd been seen. "No good," she told Daniel.

"Better stay out there anyway," he said. "In case he comes back. Can you tell if it's still storming over the mainland?"

In a moment came the reply. "Yes, but not as bad. Still dark. I don't see any lightning."

"Then we ought to have some company soon. I'm sure Jim will bring somebody over as soon as he can."

"Maybe it was that helicopter," Yolanda said. "And all he's going to report is that he didn't find anybody. No people, no little girl, no boys, no boats, nothing!"

Daniel didn't like the sound of that. "You think he'll just go back and tell them no one's here, and they'll look somewhere else?"

"I hope not! Maybe I should try to write something in the sand. He could see that from up there."

"Like what, Yo-Yo?"

"I'll think of something."

"You'd better bring another bag or two of water first! He's really sick."

Tom was rolling back and forth, saying, "Too hot, too hot, dizzy, weak, too hot. Need drink." Daniel tried to help him drink, but knew he should be working on Tom's legs so he wouldn't go into shock.

Yolanda raced down to the ocean again. But by the time she got back most of the cold water had dripped from the bag. She let the rest drip all over Tom and ran back for more. When she returned, Daniel met her at the bushes and traded her the towel for the new bag of water.

"One more time with the towel," she said. "We've got to keep him cool. Here's that spray for bug bites and sunburn. He needs it for both."

She handed it to him and ran back to douse the towel again. After Daniel had draped it over Tom, Yolanda joined them. Tom looked worse. His sunburn had turned to huge, watery blisters. And his face was flushed. He seemed delirious.

"We have to worry about infection now, too," Yolanda said. "Especially with all these bugs."

Daniel was starting to panic. "What are we going to do, Yo-Yo? We have to get him out of here! Keep watching for a boat or a plane, anything!"

She ran back out. Daniel lifted the towel and fanned Tom with it, still worried about the weak sound of his breathing. Ten minutes later, Yolanda returned. "I left a message in the sand," she said. "If they can't see that, they'd never see me either."

She knelt near Tom's head and fed him some more orange juice, a few drops at a time. He moaned and groaned. She spoke softly to him, assuring him he would be all right.

Tom seemed to do better when Yolanda was there. She

helped a lot and kept him encouraged and calm. Each time she had to leave to get more water or to soak the towel, Tom was harder for Daniel to control. He prayed she would return soon. And when the three of them were together again, he and Yolanda would pray out loud that someone would spot them.

Daniel knew that if they did not get some help for Tom soon, he would die. Daniel had worried about the lives of three people that day—first his own, then Yolanda's, and now Tom's. He knew Tom was in the most danger.

"Should we try to get him to eat something?" Daniel asked.

Tom nodded and groaned. But Yolanda shook her head and began talking to him about something else to take his mind off the subject. "Just juice," she mouthed to Daniel.

Finally they heard the helicopter again. Daniel started to bolt out of the shade, but Yolanda said, "I'll go," and left him with Tom. "That time he circled and came lower," she said when she got back. "I don't think he saw me. But he'd have to be blind not to see my message in the sand."

Tom's body seemed more stiff now. Daniel didn't know what else to do. Yolanda fed him the last of the orange juice. She spoke to him as calmly as she could and then ran to the ocean for a fresh supply of water for the towel.

Daniel was exhausted. He couldn't rub Tom's legs anymore. He was nearly in tears. He lowered his head and knelt there in the sand, wishing it was all over and that he was back on the mainland with his parents. Then he heard the helicopter again.

"My turn!" he said, and Yolanda knew he meant it. He struggled to his feet and staggered out into the open. The helicopter was landing!

Daniel waved and shouted. A Coast Guard pilot jumped from the cockpit and ran toward him. "I'm Captain Falcone. Are you Bradford?"

"Yeah."

"Are you all right?"

"Yeah."

"And is there a girl here, too? A little Mexican girl?"

"Yes, sir, she's all right, too. But my friend has sunstroke, we think."

Captain Falcone checked a slip of paper in his pocket. "That wouldn't be a Thomas Huber, would it? Twelve years old?"

"That's him. He's the one who's sick."

Daniel led the captain through the bushes to Tom. Without a word, he checked Tom's pulse, felt his forehead, and generally looked him over.

"It's sunstroke all right," he said finally. "And you're doing the right thing. But we're going to have to get him out of here. Come, help me, Daniel."

Daniel ran behind him to the helicopter where the pilot tossed him a satchel. Captain Falcone followed Daniel back to Tom with a stretcher. He knelt next to the sick boy and opened the case, producing a bottle of liquid.

"This has lots of vitamin C in it," he explained. But he couldn't get Tom to drink any.

"Let me try," Yolanda said. Within seconds, Tom was drinking.

"Help me get him on the stretcher," the captain said. "Very carefully."

Tom cried and moaned as they tried to move him. But Yolanda held his head and kept talking to him the whole time. "You're going to be OK. We're going to get you out of here and get you some help. You'll see your mom and dad before you know it. And you'll be feeling better. How's that sound?"

He nodded, and Daniel thought he tried to smile, too.

With Yolanda and Daniel on one end and Captain Falcone on the other, they carefully made their way through the trees and bushes and then down the sand. They passed the giant message Yolanda had walked off. From ground level, Daniel couldn't make out what it said. And he couldn't take the time to look more closely.

"OK, easy now," the captain said. He backed up onto the helicopter, pulling the stretcher with him. When he had Tom secure, he helped Yolanda, then Daniel, into the seat beside him, and buckled them in.

He gunned the throttle. And the powerful bird fired straight up above the island before winging toward the mainland. Daniel looked down and smiled at the job Yolanda had done on the beach.

In big letters, she had walked off the words MAY DAY, the international distress signal. With it, she had saved Tom's life. Daniel couldn't wait to see what the Hubers thought about that.

11

Back to the Mainland

Had Daniel known how close Tom had come to dying, he would have been even more scared than he was on the island. The doctor at the hospital reported that Tom had indeed gone into shock.

"What exactly does that mean?" Maryann asked.

"Basically," the doctor said, "it's a failure of the circulatory system. In other words, his blood supply system nearly collapsed. If it had, he might have died."

"What caused it?"

"From what I gather from his young friends here," the doctor said, "he was overtired. Then he fell asleep in the hot sun. He may have stirred at one point and tried to crawl into the shade, but even that was too much for him. He wound up with sunburn, sunstroke, heat exhaustion, and at least low-volume shock. If it hadn't been for the action of his friends, well, who knows?"

"Not me," Daniel said. "Yolanda was the one who knew everything about this. I dragged him out of the sun. But she told me what to do for him."

It was two days before Tom was fully awake. But somehow he remembered everything that had gone on from the time Daniel and Yolanda dragged him from the beach to the shade until he was lifted aboard the helicopter.

His mother and father were still upset about his leaving for the island without telling them. They were upset about his encouraging Daniel to help him borrow the boat. And they were upset about Yolanda's running off in the first place. They considered that the real reason he had almost been killed.

Mr. and Mrs. Huber kept avoiding the Bradfords. The whole family spent most of its time at the hospital, though, praying for Tom and keeping track of his progress. At one point, Mrs. Huber almost got into a shouting match with Mrs. Bradford.

"Don't tell me about it!" she insisted. "I don't want to know how wonderful you think Yolanda is. She was irresponsible, and that's the reason for this whole mess. Just as I predicted."

"Yolanda will be punished for what she did, but—"

"But nothing! I hold her responsible for what happened to Thomas, and indirectly you, too."

"Me?"

"I'm sure adopting her in the first place was your idea."

"Carolyn—" Mrs. Bradford was hurt.

"Lil," Mr. Bradford said, "she's upset and doesn't realize what she's saying."

"I do, too! It's your fault!"

Even her own husband disagreed with her about that. "Now, Carolyn," he said. "I know Bob and Lil are just as upset as we are about—"

"How could they be? It's not their baby who's lying in that bed!"

"I'm sure they are just as upset as we are, Carolyn. Now let's talk about this later."

Mr. Bradford took his wife down the hall so Mrs. Huber wouldn't be so agitated. "I wish she *would* talk about it now," Mrs. Bradford said. "She's wrong about Yolanda and about Mexicans, and she ought to know it."

"This isn't the time," Mr. Bradford said.

"This is the perfect time," she said. "If it weren't for Yo-Yo, her son could have died."

"She's not listening to that, and you know it," he said. "Daniel tried to tell her, and even that Coast Guard pilot tried to tell what he knew."

"But they were so relieved to have found Tom and so worried abut his condition, they weren't listening."

"And we can't blame them, Lil. Were *you* listening?"

"Not until I knew Daniel and Yolanda were all right, no."

A nurse came for them. "Mr. and Mrs. Bradford, Thomas Huber is conscious and would like to talk with you."

They hurried down the hall. The Hubers were already in the room, and it was getting crowded. "Are you sure it's all right that we're all here?" Mr. Bradford asked. With the Hubers and the Bradfords, including the patient there were eleven.

"The doctor assured me it was all right. But just for a little while."

Mrs. Huber cradled Tom's head in her hands. "How are you feeling, darling?" she asked.

"Great, now. A little weak. Real hungry. But thanks to Yolanda, I'm alive and able to eat."

His mother looked disgusted. "Thanks to Yolanda you were nearly killed."

"No, Mom. Thanks to me, she went to the island."

"What do you mean?"

"When Daniel left the beach the other day, I started teasing her. I didn't like her because I knew you didn't."

"I didn't? But, Thomas, I, I—"

"Well, if you did, Mom, you didn't act like it. I thought there was something wrong with her because she was a Mexican. And even though I didn't know what it was, I thought it would be OK to make fun of her and bother her. She got mad or scared or something and ran off. When she didn't come back, I thought she was going to go tell on me. I

68

told Theresa to run up and tell you she disappeared. Only I didn't know she really had."

"Well," his mother said. "She didn't have to go running off like that. I mean, every child has been teased—"

"Still, Mom, it was my fault. And I was feeling guilty about it. I didn't want to tell you, but I did think I should try to help find her. Then I saw Daniel at the boat launch. And he told me they had traced her to the island. Don't you see, we just had to go looking for her? We had to find her."

"No, I don't see."

"Well, I felt *I* had to anyway. And I was the one who talked Daniel into taking the boat. It was an emergency. But the storm was too strong."

Daniel spoke up. "It's a good thing Tom has some experience. He said we had to get close enough to the island so that if the storm hit, we'd be blown that way instead of into the open sea. He was right."

"Yeah, but I almost drowned, Mom. When that boat broke up, Daniel went under. I grabbed the biggest piece of the boat I could find. I was swimming and swimming against the waves, but I couldn't go any farther. I thought sure Daniel had drowned. But I kept calling for him anyway. When I thought I couldn't move or swim another stroke, he came out to get me and dragged me in. I was never so happy to see anybody in my whole life."

"Well, that's nice, Daniel," Mrs. Huber said. "And I appreciate your help, but—"

"Then when the storm let up, Daniel wanted me to go looking for Yolanda again. I didn't want him to think I was weak or lazy, but I was still so sore and tired. I made some excuse about starting a little later. I was cold and shivering. And I felt like I was coming down with something. I was glad when he started off because I knew I could get a little sleep before starting out. I don't know how long I slept."

"Pretty long," Daniel said. "At least as long as it took me to get three miles around the island. Not to mention stopping to sleep and dry my clothes besides."

"Anyway," Tom said, "long enough to get this sunburn and to get a bad fever. I woke up once, but I could hardly move. I was scared to death. My heart was beating real fast, and I couldn't breathe. I tried to take my clothes off. But all I could do was kick off my shoes. I tried to crawl to the shade, too, but I passed out. And I think I wound up in a worse spot for the sun."

"You did," Daniel said, nodding.

"I woke up again when Daniel and Yolanda dragged me into the shade. I tried to tell them what was wrong. But I couldn't make my words make sense. I was just moaning and groaning. They started pouring cold water on me and draping me with a wet towel, and feeding me orange juice. I knew I was going to be OK, even though I knew they were worried.

"It was Yolanda, Mom. She was the one whe was telling Daniel everything to do. She talked to me, encouraged me, kept me calm, and knew just what to do. She ran back and forth to the water. It must have been at least a dozen times."

Daniel nodded, and Tom continued. "She was the one who spelled out MAY DAY in the sand so the helicopter could find us. She saved my life, Mom. And I'm sorry for the way I treated her. I apologize, Yolanda, and I want to be your friend."

Yolanda smiled one of those gleaming grins of hers and took Tom's hand in both of hers. "Of course," she said. "We can be friends forever."

Mrs. Huber looked on, her eyes wet. She look as if she wanted to say something but nothing would come out. Her husband put his hands on her arms from behind. "Carolyn," he said, "I think we have some apologies of our own to make to Yolanda."

Mrs. Huber hugged Yolanda, crying. She nodded. "I know," she said. "And lots of thinking to do."

"Maybe we should talk to Bob and Lil a little more about their new daughter, too," her husband said.

Mrs. Huber squeezed Yolanda tighter. "I'm ready," she said. "Boy, am I ready."